For Aunt Al, whose strength, nurturing spirit, and love for all living things will inspire me always. I love you.

Visit us on the Web!
rhcbooks.com

Educators and librarians, for a variety of teaching tools, visit us at RHTeachersLibrarians.com

Library of Congress Cataloging-in-Publication Data is available upon request.
ISBN 978-0-593-56963-4 (trade) — ISBN 978-0-593-56964-1 (lib. bdg.) — ISBN 978-0-593-56965-8 (ebook)

The artist used Procreate to create the illustrations for this book.
The text of this book is set in 17-point Headlock.
Interior design by Elizabeth Tardiff

MANUFACTURED IN CHINA
10 9 8 7 6 5 4 3 2 1
First Edition

WITCH & WOMBAT

BY: ASHLEY BELOTE

Random House 🏠 New York

YOU NOW HAVE A WOMBAT.

They are just like cats!*

- Wombats don't play with yarn; they prefer burrowing for fun.

- Wombats don't have a history of being lucky.

- Wombats produce cube-shaped poop! They use the cubes as signposts to track their paths and mark their territory. Also, they don't use a litter box. (So watch your step. . . .)

- Wombats are bigger than cats, so they can't hide behind you.

- Wombats have small tails, so they won't be grabbing on to any broomsticks.

*Sort of.

MAYBE NO ONE WILL NOTICE. . . .

CATS RULE

They did.

Wilma the witch could not wait until tomorrow. Because tomorrow she was finally getting her very own . . .

CAT!

She had planned it all out—

the flights,

the potion brew sessions,

POOF!

the casting of spells.

But when it was
finally time to meet
her purr-fect pet . . .

A WOMBAT?!

Maybe Brewing Potions for Beginners would be better.

It wasn't.

YOU NEED TO PERCH ON THE EDGE OF MY CAULDRON.
CAT SHOULD SIT ON CAULDRON
Diagram A:
CAT--->
CAULDRON
PRACTICE WANDS
PRACTICE MAGIC HATS *RABBITS OUTSIDE*
MEOW!
CAUTION: SOMETIMES THIS CAULDRON MAKES PIRANHAS
Magician Flowers

During recess, Wilma watched all the other witches and their cats doing what witches and cats were SUPPOSED to do together.

SIGH

When she turned to look for her hat, she noticed that . . .

Wombat was gone!

OH NO . . .

Wilma had been so busy wishing she had a cat that she seemed to have wished her wombat away! She slumped to the ground, feeling bad.

That's when she noticed a trail of small cubes and remembered—wombats use their poop as land markers to track their paths!

She started to follow the trail . . .

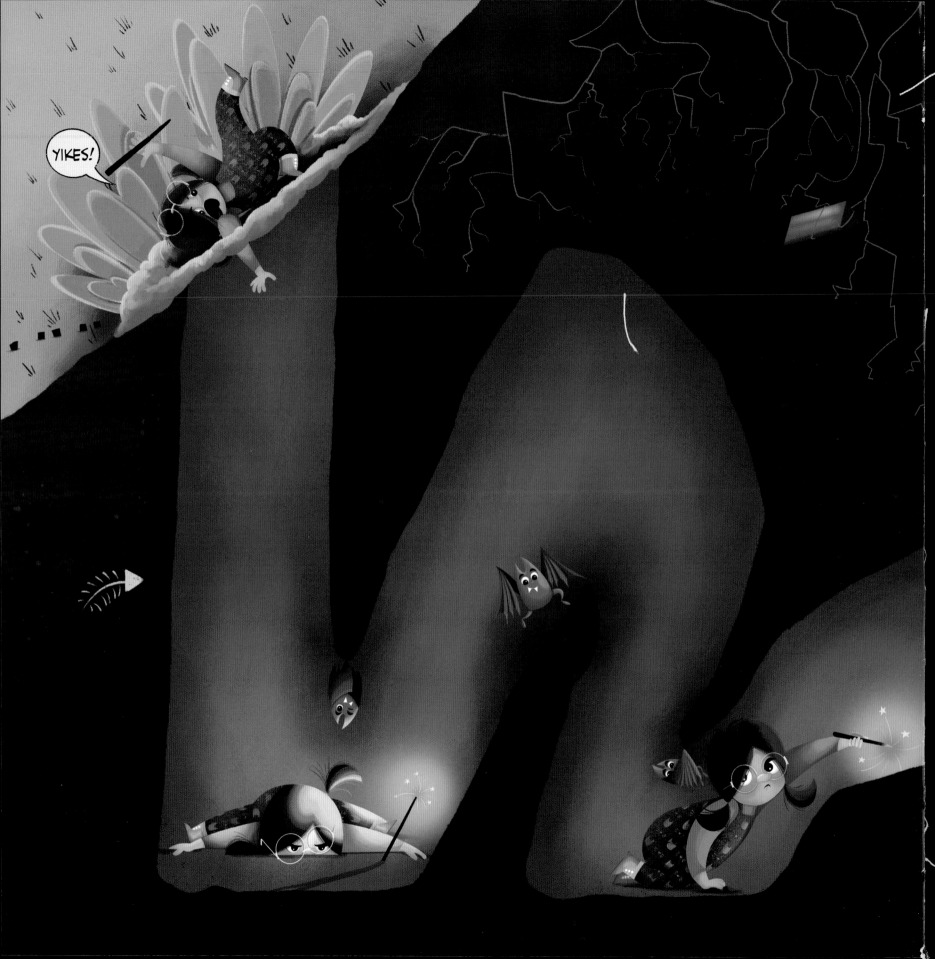

For the first time, Wilma was excited to introduce Wombat to her classmates.

And when the pet store clerk called to say they had a cat for her, Wilma replied,

Welcome!
CANDY Annex
Nap area
LADDER for Wilma
Potty CHAMBER
WOMBAT 101
DRAW ANIMALS
How-to-Burrow
Recipes
Gardener's Guide
Tricks & Treats
Pumpkin Carving
Burrowing for Beginners
Pouch Storage
Knitting 101
ART
SPELLS

CATS: *TOP ROW* FlUFFY, CUTIE PIE, PRECIOUS, SMILEY

CATS: *BOTTOM ROW* HAPPY, WOMBAT, CUDDLES, SUNNY, LARS
+ WOMBAT

MORE WOMBAT FACTS!

They can dig tunnels up to 650 feet long!

Common wombats don't chase mice;
they are herbivores—they only eat plants.

Wombats have small eyes and poor
eyesight, so their eyes don't glow and
spook you in the dark, like a cat's do.

Wombats have upside-down pouches.
What can they hide in there?